CUTE, SWEET & PETITE!

4 Pet-tacular Stories

By Amy Sky Koster

Illustrated by the Disney Storybook Art Team

A GOLDEN BOOK • NEW YORK

randomhousekids.com
ISBN 978-0-7364-3412-6
Printed in the United States of America
10 9 8 7 6 5 4 3 2 1

Sultan

A Brave Tiger for Jasmine

Sultan was a furry little tiger whose coat was white and orange with dark brown stripes. He was not very big or scary, but he always tried to be brave.

Sultan really liked to explore. When he wasn't roaming the jungle, roaring and protecting his friends . . .

. . . the little tiger could be found guarding fancy silk fabrics at the Agrabah market. *Rrraarr!* That pesky monkey better watch out for Sultan!

As a reward for his bravery, the shopkeeper fed snacks to the little tiger. Sultan enjoyed his job in the market. But more than anything else, Sultan wanted a home of his own to protect.

One lazy afternoon, Sultan snuggled up for
a catnap on a soft pile of fabrics. As the sun
warmed his face, Sultan began to drift off.
Before long, the little cub was fast asleep!

At the very same moment, Princess Jasmine was wandering through the market. She was enjoying her day of shopping—the fresh-cut flowers were lovely, and the scents of delicious spices filled the air.

Jasmine soon found herself at the silks stand. When she touched the smooth, cool fabric, her hand brushed against something warm and fluffy.

To her surprise, Jasmine discovered
Sultan sleeping among the silks! She
couldn't believe her eyes.
    Instead of being brave, the little tiger
was shy with the lovely princess.

While the shopkeeper tried to make a sale, Jasmine stared at the little cub. She forgot about the fabrics she was looking for—because all she wanted was to hug and cuddle sweet little Sultan!

Jasmine wondered if she could take the
tiger home. The merchant would miss the
little tiger, but he knew that Sultan would
have a very good life with the princess.

As they left the market, Jasmine told Sultan all about her palace. That was when Sultan realized his dream was coming true—he was going to have a home of his own!

Now Sultan proudly protects his
home in the palace and his new friends,
Aladdin and Princess Jasmine. *Rrraarr!*

Blondie

Rapunzel's Pony Dreams Big

Blondie was a little pony who had big dreams of becoming a royal horse. She couldn't wait to wear the palace's official purple bridle and fancy saddle one day!

But whenever Blondie visited the royal stables, the big horses laughed and made fun of her.

"You can't be a royal horse," they teased. "You're much too little."

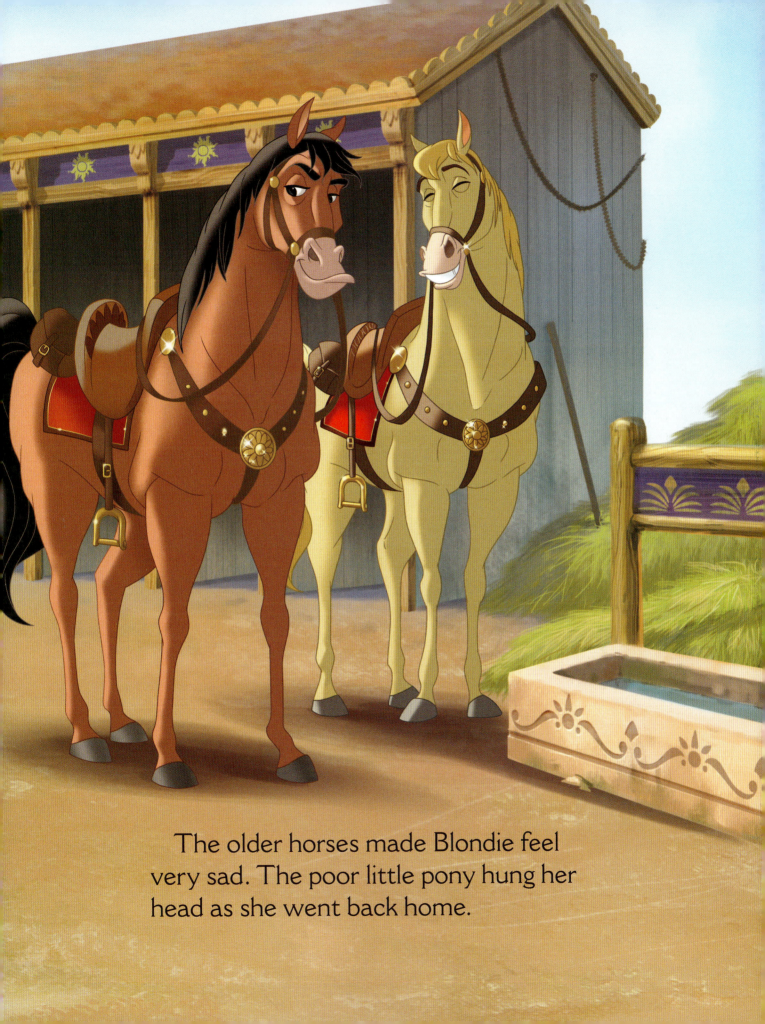

The older horses made Blondie feel
very sad. The poor little pony hung her
head as she went back home.

One very important day, Blondie got lucky.
The King and Queen were throwing a big
parade to celebrate Rapunzel's return. In the
bustle to get ready for the event, Blondie
found herself near a group of royal horses that
had been chosen to lead the parade.

Blondie had heard about Rapunzel and the legend of the lost princess. Not long before, Blondie had seen a beautiful girl enter the kingdom. She didn't know that the long-haired girl was actually Rapunzel!

Rapunzel loved parades. She liked to listen to the festive music and watch the floats roll by. The floats were decorated with beautiful flowers and majestic flags, and they were pulled along the parade route by royal horses.

Rapunzel smiled when she saw the royal horses.
As a little girl trapped in the tower, she had dreamed
of one day owning a horse. Now she could have any
horse she wanted. But Rapunzel was patient—
she was waiting for the *perfect* horse.

As Blondie marched in the parade, she got a little too excited. The pony stepped on her long mane and bumped into the horse next to her. Then she stumbled right in front of the princess!

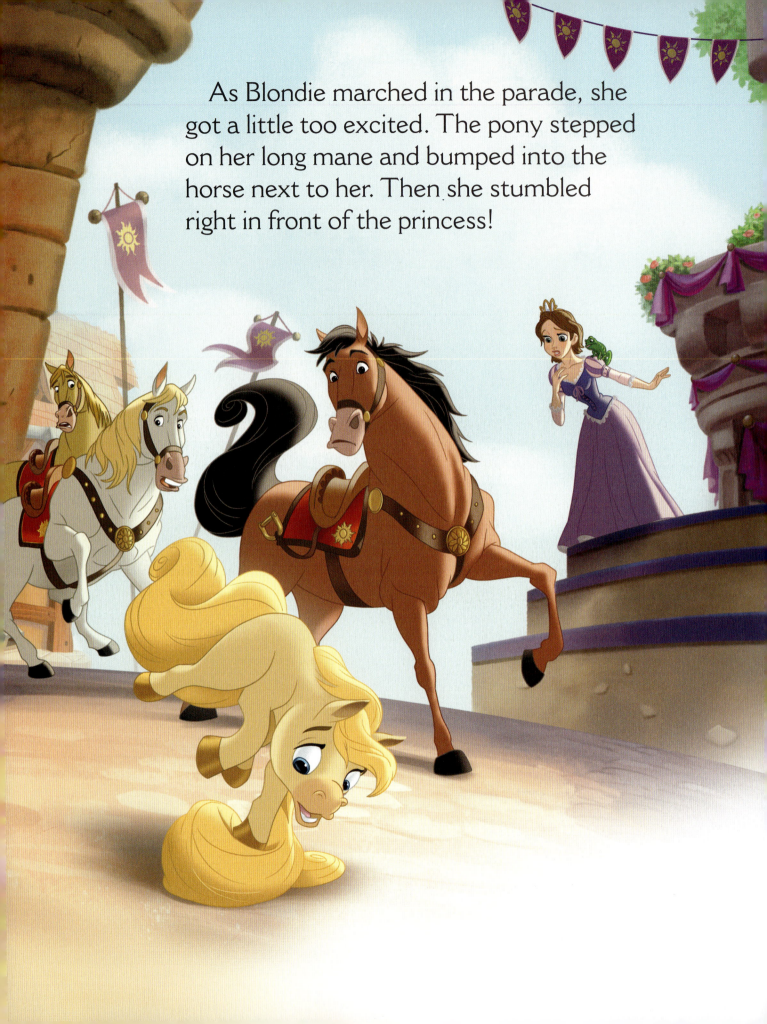

The royal horses huffed and neighed as Blondie lowered her head. She was so embarrassed!

Rapunzel slowly made her way over to the little pony. Everyone in the crowd held their breath to see what the princess would do.

Rapunzel knelt beside Blondie and made sure the little pony wasn't hurt. Then she gently started to braid Blondie's long mane. Blondie was amazed!

Rapunzel's hair used to be long and blond, just like Blondie's! Now Rapunzel's hair was short and brown. Blondie wondered if she missed having long hair to braid.

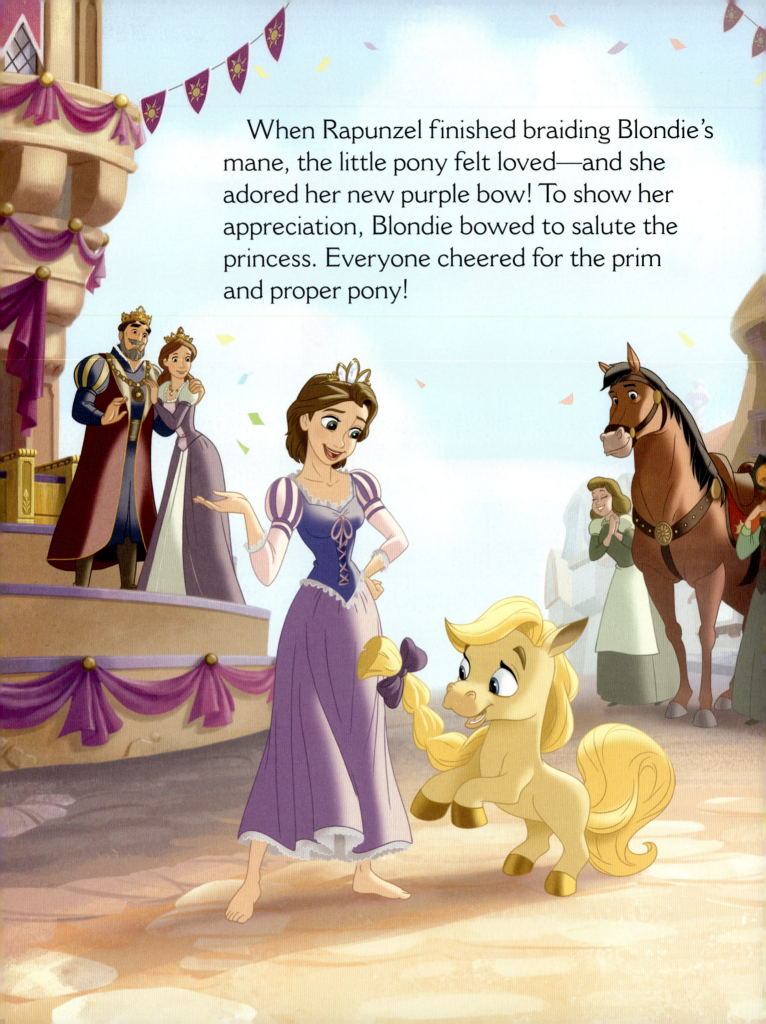

When Rapunzel finished braiding Blondie's mane, the little pony felt loved—and she adored her new purple bow! To show her appreciation, Blondie bowed to salute the princess. Everyone cheered for the prim and proper pony!

Blondie's dream came true! This little pony
is now a royal horse. More importantly, she's
one of Rapunzel's best friends, which makes
her the proudest pony in the kingdom!

Dreamy

The Kitten Who Loved to Sleep

Dreamy was a fluffy little kitten who loved to take naps. She liked to sleep in the warm morning sunshine, in the cool afternoon shade, and under the evening moon. The other kittens joked that only a prince would be able to wake her. Little did they know that it would actually take a *princess* to do the job!

Princess Aurora was no stranger to sleeping. It was known throughout the kingdom that she had once been called Sleeping Beauty—and that she had been woken from a spell with a kiss from Prince Phillip, her true love!

One sunny afternoon, Aurora was taking a walk around the palace garden with her fairy friends, Flora, Fauna, and Merryweather. The sweet scent of roses was lovely, and it took all of Aurora's willpower not to settle down for a nap. But her fairy friends weren't ready to rest.

Suddenly, Merryweather spotted something nestled in the flowers up ahead.

"Look!" Merryweather hovered above a rosy tail. "It's a lion! It's a tiger! It's a dragon!" she guessed excitedly.

Aurora thought her fairy friends were trying to play a trick on her. Soon her curiosity got the best of her, and she followed the fairies to the rosy tail. But it didn't belong to a lion, a tiger, or a dragon. It belonged to Dreamy, a fluffy little kitten!

Aurora had never seen such a beautiful kitten—she was absolutely precious! Her rosy fur shimmered in the sunshine. Her little pink nose twitched and wiggled. And her purr was soft, like beautiful music!

Aurora didn't want to disturb the kitten, but Merryweather and Fauna bounced about, trying to wake Dreamy with their magic wands. The kitten began to stir!

Dreamy noticed a breeze tickling her nose, and when the warm sun disappeared behind a cloud, she woke up. The fairies' magic had worked! The little kitten opened her eyes and saw the lovely Princess Aurora looking back at her.

Aurora was sure the surprised kitten would not be pleased. But Dreamy yawned sweetly and jumped into Aurora's arms! It was a match made in heaven.

The princess sang to Dreamy as she walked back toward the castle. Soon the kitten was purring again, and she fell fast asleep.

"You are perfect for each other, dear," said Flora, and the other fairies giggled. Aurora agreed, and she yawned, because she was sleepy, too!

Now these two beauties curl up together whenever they can. Aurora and Dreamy love to take long, luxurious naps after a busy morning. And when they wake up in the afternoon, they both like to fill their bellies with sweet snacks and yummy treats!

Bayou

A Perfect Pony for Tiana

Bayou the pony lived in a tiny country called Maldonia. She was nervous because the King and Queen wanted to take her on a trip to a big city that was far, far away. Bayou didn't know that Prince Naveen's parents were taking her to live with Princess Tiana!

Bayou boarded a big ship with Prince
Naveen's parents and set sail for America.
After a long ocean voyage, they finally
arrived in the city of New Orleans.

When Bayou was presented to Tiana, the princess couldn't believe her eyes—she thought Bayou was a perfect little pony! Tiana loved her shy smile and long, flowing tail. Bayou was excited when she found out that Tiana had a surprise for her.

It was a brand-new costume for Mardi Gras! Bayou had arrived in New Orleans just in time for the Mardi Gras parade. Everyone loved to dress up in fun outfits for the parade—it was a New Orleans tradition!

Poor Bayou wasn't used to all the noise of the
big city, and she missed her home in Maldonia.
Luckily, Tiana knew exactly what would make
Bayou feel better—a slice of apple pie she had
baked that very morning!

After her snack, Bayou began to relax.
And when she heard the music from the
parade, she couldn't help prancing a little.
Tiana smiled when she saw that Bayou
was ready to have some fun!

The Mardi Gras parade was amazing to see. But Tiana and Bayou had even more fun when they hopped aboard a float and joined the parade along with Prince Naveen and his parents!

The next day, Tiana introduced Bayou to her friend Charlotte LaBouff. Charlotte offered to let Bayou stay in the cozy stables at her family's estate. Tiana and Bayou thought that was a great idea!

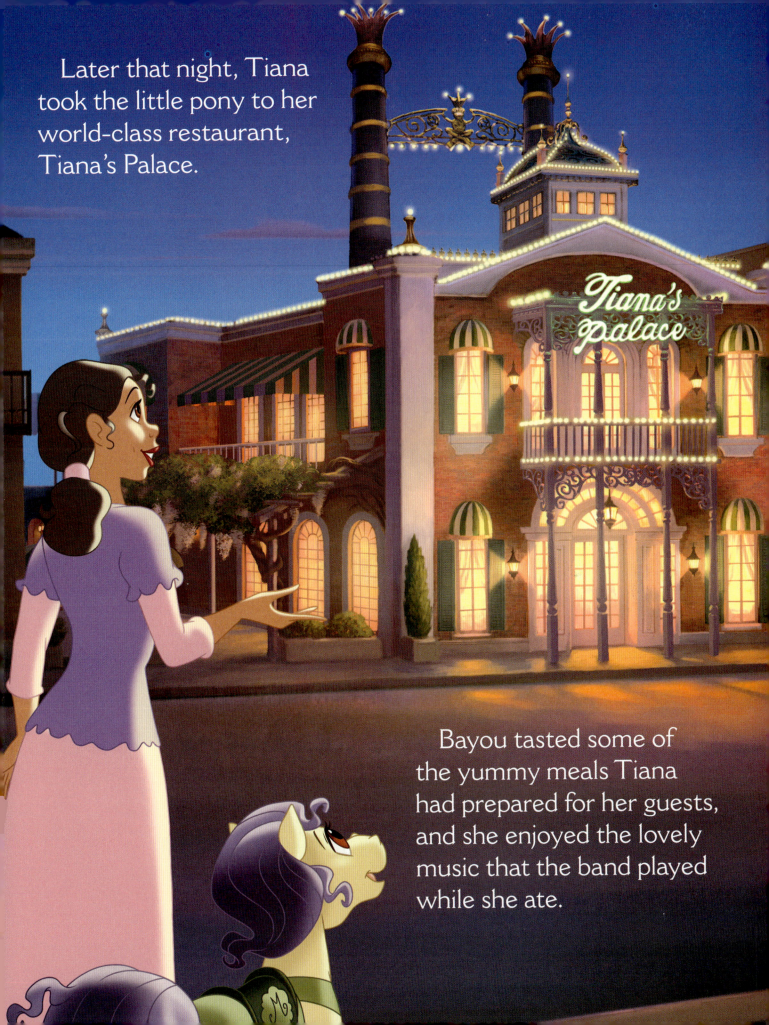

Later that night, Tiana took the little pony to her world-class restaurant, Tiana's Palace.

Tiana's Palace

Bayou tasted some of the yummy meals Tiana had prepared for her guests, and she enjoyed the lovely music that the band played while she ate.

Now Bayou adores everything about New Orleans. She loves the food, enjoys the parades, and likes dressing up in costumes. But most of all, Bayou loves spending time with Tiana, her new best friend!